This edition published by Mantra Lingua Ltd,
Global House, 303 Ballards Lane, London N12 8NP, UK
www.mantralingua.com

烏鴉王

一個韓國民間故事

The Crow King

A Korean Folk Story

by Lee Joo-Hye
Illustrated by Han Byung-Ho
Retold in English by Enebor Attard

Cantonese translation by Sylvia Denham

很久以前，在烏鴉出沒的地帶有一個用恐怖手腕統治的烏鴉王，
牠會隨意掠殺任何人，根本沒有人可以阻止牠。
有一天，當一對男女回家時，烏鴉王出現，
牠威猛下撲，一下子便抓著那女人，
然後飛到無人到過的高峻山巔去。

A long time ago, in the land of the crows, there lived a king who ruled with terror.
He would take anyone he liked and no-one could stop him.
One day, a man and woman were going home when the Crow King came.
In one giant swoop he grabbed the woman and flew away to the steep and
lofty peaks where no human had ever been.

即使地勢險峻幽暗和處身於朦朧的白霧中，
那個男人發誓他一定要尋回那女人。

The man swore that he would find the woman even though the land was rough and gloomy, and he could barely see through the white mist.

他在山上越爬越高，直至他來到一間住著一個隱居逸士的小屋。
「不要再爬了，」她警告道，「在你之前有很多人都試過。」
那男人說他絕不畏懼，因爲他的愛是真誠的。
「年青人，你將會需要勇氣才會堅強，」那隱士說。
「你必須打開十二扇門才能找到她，而每一扇門都有烏鴉監視著，等著殺害你！切記無論發生什麼事，即使是邪惡也會有終結的。」
她跟著便從小屋拿出一些米餅，然後說道：
「用這些去哄騙烏鴉上當吧。」

He climbed higher and higher until he came to a hut where a hermit lived.
"Go no further," she warned. "Many have tried before you."
The man said he was not frightened, for his love was true.
"Young man, you will need courage to be strong," the hermit said. "Twelve doors must you open to find her and at each door the crows watch, waiting to kill you! Remember, no matter what happens, even evil has an end." Then, bringing some rice cakes from her hut, she said, "Here, take these to trick the crows."

風刮得更勁，雨下得更大，天色非常漆黑，
那男人還以為天空已經塌下來了。他一步一步的向上爬，
直到他看到一座有十二扇門的堡壘，到處都是烏鴉－
飛翔著、啄食著、吱叫著、觀望著－
望著這愚蠢的男人漠視前面的危險。

The winds blew wilder, the rain fell harder. It was so dark that the man thought
the sky had fallen down. Step by step the man climbed until he saw the fortress
of a dozen doors with crows everywhere - flying, pecking, screeching,
watching - watching this foolish man ignore the danger ahead.

到了第一扇門，那男人向烏鴉顯示一塊米餅，然後將它扔到遠處。
雀鳥們不再理會他，並衝向那米餅，而他則悄悄地穿過門口走到第二扇門。
他這樣地重復又重復，每一次烏鴉們都不理會他。

At the first door the man showed the crows one rice cake and flung it far away.
The birds ignored him and rushed to the cake while the man quietly slipped through to the
second door. He did this over and over again and each time the crows ignored him.

當他開啓第十二扇門時，他看到在一個湖的中央有一間屋。
他呼叫那個女人，她便走出來歡欣地擁抱他。
「快，」她說，「那兇殘的烏鴉王很快便會回來。」

Opening the twelfth door the man saw a house in the middle of a lake.
He called to the woman who rushed out and hugged him with joy.
"Hurry," she said, "the monster Crow King will be back very soon."

屋內有一把劍，劍柄有一條龍，另外還有一對鞋。
「快，」她說，「這些都是屬於那猛獸的，你一定要拿走它們。」
但是那把劍太重，鞋子也太大了。
那個女人將一個水瓶裝滿了湖水，然後說：「飲下這藥劑，
它會給你勇氣的。」

Inside was a huge sword with a dragon handle and a pair of shoes.
"Quick," she said, "these belong to the monster and you must take them."
But the sword was too heavy and the shoes were too big.
Filling a jug with water from the lake, the woman cried, "Drink this tonic,
it will give you courage."

那男人記得隱士所說的話，於是便把那苦澀的液體飲了，
他可以感覺到自己變得更巨大和更輕盈，他穿上鞋子，
竟然可以輕鬆地舞動和踢雙腳，他拿起那把劍，
它就好像竹枝一樣的輕巧，他感覺到一條龍的靈性進入他的心間。
他一點也不害怕。

The man recalled what the hermit said and drank the bitter liquid.
He could feel himself growing bigger and lighter. He put on the shoes
and his feet danced and kicked with ease. The sword he lifted was
as light as a bamboo branch and he felt the spirit of the dragon
enter his heart.
He was not afraid.

過了一陣子，牠們便到來，首先是烏鴉王，跟著便是他的隨從烏鴉，牠們都尖叫和唾罵。

They came a moment later. First the Crow King, then his follower crows, shrieking and spitting.

「你以為你可以殺我嗎？」烏鴉王目露凶光地說，「你太細小和太柔弱，實在不足為患。」牠轉頭向牠的隨從說：「烏鴉們，殺了他。」

"So, you think you can kill me, do you?" said the Crow King, his eyes wild with anger. "You are too small and weak to bother with." Turning to his followers, he said, "Crows, kill him."

那些烏鴉戰士跳向那男人，他勇敢地揮動他的劍。

The warrior crows hopped towards the man who swished his sword bravely.

當烏鴉們看到那個男人就好像一條龍一樣地戰鬥，牠們都感到驚訝，那男人毫不留情地將烏鴉們殺死，跟著…

Then to their astonishment the man fought like a dragon, killing them without mercy, until...

烏鴉王用一枝矛攻擊他，那男人跳起擋住攻擊。

the Crow King charged at him with a lance. The man leapt to block the charge.

他斬下烏鴉王的左臂，跟著斬牠的右臂，
但是它們立即便奇怪地又生長出來。

He cut off the Crow King's left arm, then his right arm.
But to his amazement they grew back immediately.

「哦，」烏鴉王吼叫道，「你仍然以為你可以殺我嗎？」
那男人斬下牠的翅膀，但它很快又重新長出來，
他的勇氣開始動搖了。

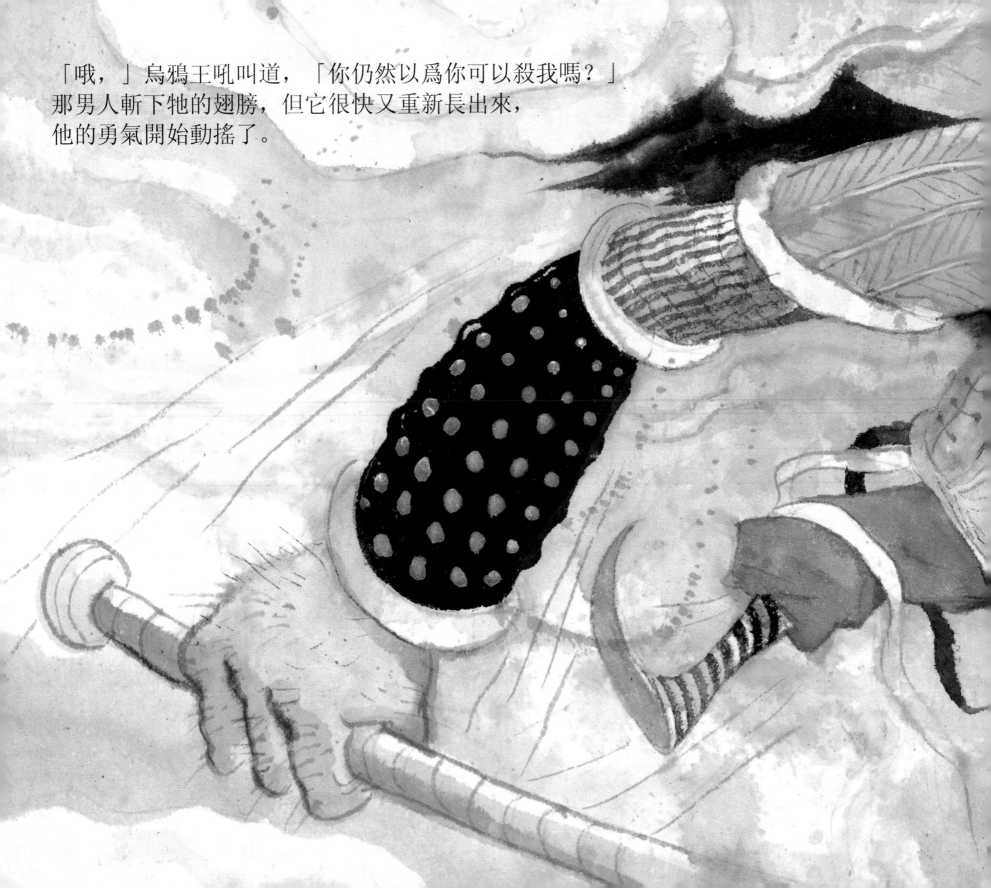

"So," bellowed the Crow King, "do you still think you can kill me?"
The man chopped off a wing but when it grew back again his courage began to fade.

"His head," shouted the woman, quickly gathering a basket of ash. "No new head can be so evil."
And with a final swipe the man chopped off the Crow King's head. The other crows stopped
clawing, they stopped shrieking. For once there was silence everywhere.
The man and woman gathered the sword and shoes. They filled the jug with more water and left
the kingdom of crows, praying that a new gentler king would be found.

「牠的頭，」那個女人叫道，跟著很快地收集一籠灰燼，
「任何新的頭都不會這樣的邪惡的。」
那男人最後一次揮劍斬下烏鴉王的頭，其他的烏鴉都停止張牙舞爪，
牠們停止尖叫著，終於寂靜一片。
那對男女緊握那把劍和鞋子，他們將水瓶載滿湖水後便離開烏鴉的王國，
並祈求新的烏鴉王會比較溫和仁慈。